Derek and Angela McMillan

Published 2022

Introduction

These stories are entertaining short fiction for your amusement. Some of them were originally published in the American Magazine *Page and Spine.*

Some of them are flash fiction which means they are under 1000 words in length. It you are interested in trying your hand at flash fiction you can have a look at https://worthingflash.blogspot.com where there are a number of examples. The next thing to do is to write your own flash fiction and email it to worthingflash@gmail.com so it can be considered for the blog.

What I am looking for in flash fiction is brevity or brev for short. Write your story and then read through it to see if you could express yourself more succinctly. With practice you will be able to do this in your head.

I also advise checking your spelling. This is to save time for the editor. I am the editor of #worthingflash.

Derek McMillan

The Twittens of Durrington

In 1875, Eric Twitten retired from his job as a saggar maker's bottom knocker and the family settled in Potter's Field in Durrington.

He spent a lot of his time exploring the small alleyways around Durrington which are popularly referred to as "twittens" to this day.

He would always carry a stout walking stick.

On a Friday evening he was walking home in the twilight. His lantern was reflected in two bright malevolent eyes.

He had no time to decide whether he was frightened or brave because a large dark shape, the owner of the eyes, leapt up at his throat, apparently intending to rip it out using its teeth.

Eric beat the feral dog off with his stout stick and he raised it to give the miscreant a good hiding for its trouble.

Then he saw in the dim lamplight, the dog which was not quite as large as he had thought, though big enough, was cowering as if to make himself disappear into the ground. It is literally impossible to be angry with a dog in this position.

Eric sighed. The dog was clearly malnourished and he could almost, but not quite, forgive its desire to make a meal of Eric.

He was close to Potter's Field by now. He stepped over the crouching dog and went on his way home. He could not resist looking behind him and saw the dog was following at a respectful distance.

"Oh, come on, boy. I think you need a wash and a good meal don't you?"

He was tossing up between "Grip", "Fang" or "Wolf" as a name for his new best friend when he arrived home and his wife, Peggy solved the problem for him.

"Eric Twitten, you are not bringing that ragamuffin in here."

"Ragamuffin" was a suitably rough name for a tough dog, he thought.

Eventually, Peggy let him take Ragamuffin into the back garden and wash him down. She didn't even object to the fact Eric wanted to use warm water. Think of the expense!

When Ragamuffin was clean and dry, Peggy permitted him into the kitchen where he stretched out in front of the fire as if he owned it.

There was no such thing as dog food. Ragamuffin had to have table scraps and be grateful. A warm house and food was preferable to a cold alleyway and slow starvation he thought.

"You stay in the kitchen Ragamuffin. It's warm enough for you no doubt," said Peggy.

She cuffed Ragamuffin's head but it wasn't meant to hurt.

She was surprised, but not very surprised, to find the weight of a ragamuffin sneaking into their bed at dead of night.

She upped and returned him to the kitchen. She did it three times but exhaustion got the better of her in the end.

Next day, Eric went out to buy a dog lead.

Ragamuffin was not happy with it and had a good go at chewing it. There were studs and they were a bit too much for his teeth so it remained intact. This meant Eric could take him with him on his daily walks.

Ragamuffin was not at all sure at first. He was used to wandering whither he would. The deal-breaker for him was that wherever Eric went, he always came back to the comfortable kitchen and the welcoming fire.

Eric's itinerary was well-known so it was not long before two local ne'er-do-wells took it into their heads to waylay him. They had reckoned without his new best friend.

"Hand over your money."

"I don't carry money unless I'm shopping and the wife does that."

"We'll have that watch off you then."

"I have no time for you," Eric said.

"I've got a knife."

"Well that puts a different complexion on matters."

Eric was about to hand over the watch and Ragamuffin wasn't having that. Many dogs give a low growl or indeed a lot of loud barking when about to attack. Ragamuffin couldn't be bothered.

It is very hard to hold a knife when a very large dog has decided on your wrist for lunch.

Taking heart, Eric assailed his assailants with his stick and they ran away with their metaphorical tails between their legs.

Ragamuffin got a nice steak out of this which only seemed right and proper. Nobody ever impeded Eric from that day onwards.

The End

Dave's Contraption

"I am not using it to take lobsters to the moon," was all Dave ever said about the contraption he was making in the shed. He was not a talkative chap, Dave.

He worked as a surly shop-assistant in McTavish's fish shop. Old man McTavish liked his shop-assistants surly. "They come here to buy fish, not to pass the time of day. And you wouldn't want to pass the time of day with those half-wits anyway." was his considered opinion on the matter.

So time went by and Dave got on with constructing his contraption. People noticed parts arriving at the cottage, electronic parts, metal parts and most intriguing specialist latex parts. He was buying the best, it was assumed in the village, that a surly shop-assistant's salary could buy.

Dave had lived in in Homely Cottage ever since his parents had died. I remember asking old Phil, who was acknowledged to be the village expert on everything, about Dave's parents.

"Well they married for love, as people do. Then they settled down to forty seven years of tearing strips off each other. Neighbours couldn't help hearing their rows. Now as you know village folk are fond of knowing everybody's business but people passing in the street could pick up Dave's dad's opinion of Dave's mum and vice versa.

"I have always assumed that Dave is so good at the surliness because of his upbringing but he has become significantly surlier since he has been in Homely Cottage all on his own."

After the completion and installation of the contraption in Homely Cottage, somebody overheard a conversation in the cottage apparently between Dave and a Mr Day. Old Phil's theory on this was that Dave had been counting out the tablets he was supposed to take for his surliness, some singularly ineffective remedy in my opinion and he simply referred to the fact that he had "missed a day."

Dave had a great habit of talking to himself which was fortunate because nobody else was interested in talking to him. The fifteenth time he met you with abuse or a stony silence you tended to get the message. People didn't think anything about the voices coming from Homely Cottage although they did notice that they seemed to be raised in anger more often of late.

Some joker had the wheeze of putting a cuddly toy lobster outside Dave's door. This caused some hilarity because his denial of any lobster involvement in his contraption was well-known. Unfortunately Dave tripped over the little plaything and turned the street blue with his invective against the person or persons unknown who deposited the lobster..

I don't know if this would be the time to admit that I was the culprit. No perhaps not.

The upshot of this was that his Aunt Edith came to stay with Dave because his broken ankle was preventing him from his accustomed activities.

While she was there, she accidentally, well perhaps not all that accidentally, turned on Dave's contraption.

"That was a bloody stupid thing to do." said a voice from the contraption.

"You're a fine one to talk. If I had a pound for every stupid thing you've done I would be rich." said a different voice.

The exchange became more and more heated and it became apparent that parts of the contraption were capable of landing blows on other parts of it which then apparently cried out with pain when it did so.

So at last we found out the secret of Dave's contraption. Missing his parents, he had constructed a rowing machine.

The end

Pickle

"I think I've got myself into a bit of a pickle, Lance."

My brother, Gordon, is the only person outside the world of PG Woodhouse who could get himself into "a bit of a pickle." He had been playing away from home and needed a couple of days to 'sort everything out' as he put it. I did not rate his chances very highly.

"The thing is, Lance, I need a bit of a favour."

"Yes," I said cautiously.

"You see, I can't be seen to be away from work. I've run out of sick leave and in any case Miriam (that is Gordon's wife) can't know I am away."

Although we are not identical or even twins we do look sufficiently alike to be mistaken for each other.

"How can I help?"

"That's very good of you," (well it certainly was) "I need you to stand in for me for a couple of days max."

"Miriam?" I began.

"Well I think you could say you have a touch of that bug that's going around which gives you a sore throat so you will be sleeping in the spare room to save her getting it, if you see what I mean."

We discussed this for some time but in the end I went along with it.

Gordon trained as a teacher (he really did) at the same College of Education as I attended. He emailed me all his lesson plans and we agreed that I would take over from him on Monday while he went off to sort out his dilemma.

Lady Bügg High School has 1600 pupils and about 150 staff. I gave the staffroom a miss and went to Gordon's form room on the first floor in D block, room number 110.

I got there all right and it said "MR BATES" on the door for confirmation.

There was a teacher in occupation with a year 7 class. He stood up and he walked over to me peevishly.

"Gordon. You've forgotten already that we agreed to swap rooms for registration this morning."

"Oh I am terribly sorry. Which room are my class in?"

"Mine of course."

When I continued to look vague, he pointed across the corridor to his room.

"Gordon, have you been overworking?" he asked, "your voice really sounds bad, it's that sore throat virus I didn't realise it rotted the brain too."

 I went to register a form I had never seen before.

"Adamson," I said confidently.

"Are you doing the register today?" the child known as Adamson made this unexpected inquiry.

"You usually just look around the room and fill the ticks in." he explained.

"You can fill the ticks in," I said, handing him the register.

"Are you allowed to do that?"

Of course not but it was Gordon's problem not mine.

I had a maths class back in my "own" room. Try teaching a class when you don't know their names. No worse, try it with a class who think you **do** know their names.

"Were you called Master Bates when you were at school, sir?"

Nobody has ever asked me that before.

"I see the beauty and elegance of quadratic equations are lost on you."

One or two laughed in a world-weary sort of way. Clearly my brother has been stealing my lines too. However, there were no more cheeky questions.

I saw from Gordon's notes that the next class was 9K2, a "challenging" one.

A way to master the problem of long-division is to sit in the back row and make farting noises. This was the tactic of a young man who I found out was called Eliot.

"Will you send Eliot to the sin bin?" one asked. From their air of anticipation I guessed that Eliot usually made a fuss about this.

Instead, I talked him through the content of the lesson. The others were listening. By the end of the lesson he said, "I quite like the sin bin you know." I was overwhelmed by his gratitude.

I had tuna sandwiches in room 110 for lunch. I settled down to the Guardian crossword, an Arucaria. 5 down was "Tennis match without score can lead to romance(4,6)." I thought of Gordon's bit of a pickle as I filled in "Love Affair".

The next period was a free period. It meant I had to go to the staffroom to check if I had a cover lesson.

"What are you doing, Gordon?"

"Checking if I'm on cover."

"Surely to goodness you know the cover supervisors do all that crap these days," he added. I exited the staffroom as soon as was reasonable and went for a stroll.

The last lesson was in the computer room. The lesson was already online so there was no marking for me and plenty for Gordon as the pupils worked through his lesson on the computer. I could see their screens on a master screen at the front of the room. Usefully, the name of the pupil also appeared.

I found out one called Rabbits was flipping between the lesson and a chatroom.

"Is old Bates shagging Miss Honeyball?"

Rabbits didn't know and I arranged to have a little word with him after the lesson.

Cheri Honeyball was another member of staff and if the rumour was true then clearly Gordon wasn't playing very far away from home.

The day ended. I had succeeded in outfoxing the pupils but arousing the suspicions of two members of staff. Their likely suspicion was that old Bates was losing his marbles.

I couldn't deceive Miriam but that didn't bother me. When I got to Gordon's home, Miriam was ready with two glasses of wine and an open invitation. Gordon wasn't the only one who was playing away.

The end

Robbers

There were people in the house when we arrived home. We came into the living room and they were sitting there as bold as brass on *our* sofa. One of them was smoking. *SMOKING* in the house! He was ignoring the absence of ash trays and using the carpet instead. He seemed at home.

"Robbers!" shouted Angelina.

The couple looked at us in some surprise.

"I think you are the robbers. What are you doing in our house?"

"This is our house," I said with what I considered admirable calm. "We have the keys. We live here."

"No," said the man with some aggression. "We bought the house. We moved in today."

"Is this your furniture?"

"No. The house was sold furnished."

"Including the books?"

"Including the books but we'll be getting rid of that rubbish I'm sure."

"Why are the books still here?"

"Sadly, the old couple who lived here were both killed. We bought it from their nephew Albert for a very reasonable price."

He showed us the paperwork. My scapegrace of a nephew had indeed sold our house to them. I was going to have a few words with Albert. No doubt he had spent it all on booze and drugs.

Angelina was crying by now. The couple of robbers seemed very calm considering the circumstances.

The man (I never learnt his name) said, "Come and have a look in the back garden." He pointed me towards my own back door.

I have had to walk with a stick since the old war wound I sustained in Grosvenor Square in the anti Vietnam war protest so I took my time ambling to the back door..

When Angelina and I were in the garden we stopped short.

In the middle of our lawn, our once beautiful lawn I might add, two graves had been dug. This was not what I had been looking forward to!

The man had a knife in his hand.

"The owners don't seem to be dead. We can soon put that right."

I have never tried disarming a knife man with a knobbly stick before but I gave it a go. The stick made a satisfying 'thwack' sound when it contacted his wrist.

He dropped the knife.

His companion wailed like a banshee which was her only contribution to the proceedings..

We both went for the knife. I got it first.

I was about to rearrange his face when I was stopped by a shout.

"Uncle Leo, calm down for chrissakes. It was just a little joke."

The man and his companion were grinning.

"April Fool," he said with glee.

I ordered them off the premises.

They went. I was still holding the knife.

Angelina took the knife from me and we went inside for a nice cup of tea. My nephew Albert is definitely off the Christmas list from now on.

The end.

Signs

"Anton, I don't believe in horoscopes."

"You are a typical Capricorn, Simon."

"Seven billion people on this planet. That means about 580 million people are Capricorn. So this horoscope applies to all of them?"

"What does it say?" he sighed.

"One horoscope tells me to "Connect with people on a deep level, Capricorn. Much of your focus is on emotional security. Make sure your home is a sanctuary where you feel comfortable being exactly who you are. Demonstrate patience and understanding through your words and actions.'"

"But another tells me 'You're likely to be craving a fantastical adventure out into greener pastures today, Capricorn. You may find yourself searching for foreign rentals or dreaming up a new life altogether.' "

"Do you really think over half a billion people are going to want to go abroad while making their home a sanctuary? The one in the paper is more precise. 'A new person is going to come into your life and change it forever.'

"That's where you're wrong Simon. You look at three different horoscopes and that's bound to muddy the waters. Just focus on one."

"The one in the paper?"

"That will do. But somebody new isn't going to come into your life here."

"Is this an excuse to go down to Wetherspoons?"

"Yes."

Spoons was not too crowded on a school night. Looking round the bar I realised I knew everybody there.

The evening was drawing to a close when a stranger walked in to the bar.

Her name was Morganna. She was a clairvoyant. I kept a straight face.

"I'm usually quite cheerful so people hit me because they want to strike a happy medium. You can laugh now, I know you want to."

We gave a polite laugh.

"Are you connected with the letter 'S'?" she asked me.

"Yes," I said looking around to see if I had my initials on anything.

"You haven't," she said, "most people are connected with a letter somehow, it's the oldest trick in the book."

"What book is that?" asked Anton.

"The Egyptian Book of the Dead," she said seriously.

Anton said he had a cat to look after or it may have been a dog. Anyway he left us alone.

There was just time for one more drink before closing time.

That was that for the evening but we swapped phone numbers.

"We could go for a meal or a séance if you prefer," I said.

"Oh, a meal is cheaper and a séance is work for me," she smiled.

I thought about it for a day or so but I had promised Anton to follow this through wherever it led. I phoned the number.

We dined at an unpretentious Asian Fusion restaurant. The food was excellent as I recalled.

"Oh you've been here before?"

"I er well my wife and I, my late wife and I, we used to come here quite a bit."

I could almost see her ears prick up at the sound of a bereavement. Her voice went down a semitone.

"Do you want to talk about her?"

Of course I did. I decided her name was Caroline and she had been fond of horses and gerbils. I knew all about her musical tastes and the books she liked. Conveniently they were all books I had read.

Morganna was saddened by the story.

"How did Caroline die?"

"It was very sudden, a hit and run driver. She didn't stand a chance. You read about these things but never expect them to happen to you."

"It must have been terrible for you."

"Let's talk about other things," I said.

We did but the talk kept drifting back to Caroline.

The next day I got a phone call.

"This is Morganna, Simon. I think I've got a message for you from the other side. I know you are a bit of a skeptic but could you come around tomorrow evening. It'll be a private séance and I'll cook spaghetti bolognese. Please do come, Simon."

"You had me at spag bol. What time?"

"About eight. I will look forward to it."

I arrived with a bottle of Co-op Cabernet Sauvignon. The cooking smells from the kitchen were enticing and I rather hoped we were eating pre-seance rather than post. We were.

The room was surprisingly normal. I don't know what I was expecting: black cat, broomstick, cauldron, that kind of thing.

We chatted generally but kept reverting to the subject of Caroline and the awful way she died. I hope I looked suitably upset.

When it was time for the séance, Morganna turned the lights down and we held hands. I felt silly to be honest.

Then suddenly Morganna went into a trance. There was a voice from the ether. It really was very well done.

"Is that Simon?"

"Yes."

"Do you remember that day trip we had to Paris? You were so taken with the place, you remember. There were no laws against dogs fouling up the streets and you trod in something a little Shih tzu had left on the pavement. Do you remember?"

I was nodding like an idiot.

"It is lovely here, Simon. The dogs are very well behaved. So are the owners. It's sunny and bright and full of flowers and trees and the only thing I miss is you. You must feel that."

Then the voice changed. It became menacing and harsh.

"Simon Trent. My friend Google says you were never married. There never was a Caroline just a mean little trick."

Morganna opened her eyes. They were blazing with anger.

"The door is over there," she said.

I took the hint.

The End

The Future

"The project involves looking forward in time 200 years to witness the election. We can access the internet of the future," Tilly began, "I have done a reconnaissance and it seems that elections to the parliament are annual. First however I think we need to solicit the opinions of Wolf-Dietrich von Raitenau who has a unique perspective on democracy.

The graveyard of St Sebastian was not a welcoming venue at the best of times and Wolf-Dietrich was as vexed as he always was when he had been snatched from a dream of Salome Alt. Still he agreed to accompany them on this fact-finding mission.

There was still a Queen of England which Wolf-Dietrich thought right and proper. In the pictures, the Queen looked very young. By accessing Google Tilly was able to ascertain that the Queen the previous year had been a different person and the year before yet another. She had about as much power as the Queen of the May, no matter what some folks say.

Buckingham Palace had been turned into council flats and one of them was always reserved for the Queen.

Black Rod had been retired and given a stick to play with. There was no summoning of the commons to the Lords.

"Why is that?" Asked Wolf-Dietrich

"They abolished the House of Lords," said Xavier.

Wolf-Dietrich just shook his head at that.

"Have you looked at the moon?" asked Tilly.

They looked. It was a waxing gibbous moon and it was green.

"The green is a distant relative of wheat adapted to the lunar conditions. Most of it is under glass and will be harvested. There will be 'Luna Pops' on sale in the shops soon although most of the harvest will go to feed the 50,000-strong population of lunatics. That's what they call themselves." Tilly insisted. "The rest of the wheat you can see is trying to survive in the lunar atmosphere and contributing to the terraforming of the moon. It will be OK for humans to live on the surface in another hundred years."

"Now about the election we are here to observe." Wolf-Dietrich was keen to keep his companions on track.

"There are no news channels. They were continually being disproved on social media so 80 years ago a woman known only as 'Alice' developed an application which could create a bot..." Tilly began

"a bot is..."Xavier interrupted

"I know what a bot is." said Wolf-Dietrich, somewhat surprisingly

"Anyway this bot will filter the facts for you according to your own predilections. I have chosen to focus on this election but there is surprisingly little coverage."

Tilly added,"This is because there are no political parties."

"They were abolished?" asked Wolf-Dietrich with altogether too much relish.

"No .They withered away. There were no careers to be made in politics. The ten MPs only get the average wage of a skilled worker – no expenses. And they can only stand once. Next year a different ten take their place.

"And what do they do?"

"The real decisions are taken by the general public who can promulgate and then vote on propositions. They verify the proposals. Or negate them of course.

"For example?" Wolf-Dietrich asked.

It was Xavier who answered. "They rejected a proposal to limit the number of whales killed in the North Sea."

"Mind you," added Tilly, "that was only because it contradicted a recent motion to ban whale fishing altogether which had a larger vote.".

"So all you have told me is this. You have abolished the monarchy and replaced it with a show. You have scrapped the House of Lords and replaced it with nothing. And these ten men..." Wolf-Dietrich thundered.

"Six of them are women" Tilly interrupted.

"These ten people are just a rubber stamp for the will of the people? You have effectively abolished the state. Where is the chance for a strong leader to emerge in all this mess?"

"You have analysed the situation and concluded that there is no way for autocracy to gain the upper hand?" asked Tilly quietly.

"You could say that," Sensing a trap, Wolf-Dietrich answered cautiously.

"What about a military coup?" asked Xavier.

Wolf-Dietrich's eyes lit up but Tilly had done her homework on this too.

"There was a public inquiry in which it came out that there were more admirals than battleships and more generals than tanks..."

"What are tanks?"

Tilly brought up some pictures and Wolf-Dietrich was fascinated for half an hour with the potential of this battlefield weapon. He briefly imagined himself driving the Bavarians back with a division of tanks.

"Most of the officers were pensioned off. You can still read their blogs complaining that the army is no career for a gentleman these days. Their main complaint is that the officers are now elected for a fixed term and then have to serve in the ranks."

"That is utterly ludicrous. Officers require specialised skills."

"And it is from the people with specialised skills that the officers are elected. Regiments regularly send NCOs for training and the officer class is no longer recruited from the 'Hooray Henries'. So the chances of a coup are greatly reduced."

From the Diary of Wolf-Dietrich von Raitenau

I will be pleased to get back to the old certainties of my life in Salzburg. It was good to spend time with my young friends but the world they showed me seemed horrific. Rank and file soldiers are not fit to take decisions and the common people are not fit to frame referendum questions.

Of course Tilly is right in saying that they are better educated and better informed than at any time in history and I must put my faith in that. "Blessed are the poor" but being blessed and the recipients of charity is one thing. Putting power in their hands is another!

The end

The Project

"The Project" was a cafe and food bank. It was the brain child of old Ron Harbinger who had got together the funding from local charities and the Council. A condition of the Council's involvement was that there was a councillor on the committee.

Councillor Woolley was a new member of the committee but his first remark drew attention.

"I don't think people who are getting handouts should be sitting with people who are having a meal."

When everybody else laughed he realised they thought he was joking so he just smiled and said nothing else for the duration of the meeting.

He had a coffee with old Ron afterwards.

"I think it is just marvellous that the community is providing this wonderful service."

"It's all your fault, you know," Ron said quietly.

"Pardon."

"Before your wonderful government, people didn't need so many marvellous food banks did they?"

"I don't know."

Old Ron looked him in the eye and said, "Yes you do."

Councillor Woolley finished his coffee.

…

"Tony, can you come into my office for a minute?" It wasn't a question. Not from Malcolm Blunt, CEO of Blunt Electronics.

Tony Woolley sat down and tried to look unworried.

"Listen, Tony. You have quite a rapport with your section, a certain je ne sait quoi."

Blunt always threw the French Dictionary at him when he was up to something shady.

"There will be a few changes. Entre nous we are going to have a merger, well more properly a takeover, with Gestronics and one or two people will have to go as we slim down the company. You understand?"

"And you would like me to talk to them?"

"I have a list here. Of course you can assure them that there is a generous redundancy package."

Tony Woolley googled Gestronics. The company website painted them as a caring, environmentally friendly family business. The news channels called them "ruthless asset-strippers."

He called in the members of his section one at a time to tell them about the generous redundancy package. Some of them even thanked him.

The next day Mr Blunt was not in the office. Mr Woolley had to stand in for him.

He had a phone call which showed up on the screen as "B Young Gestronics."

"Hi Bazza here, I thought you'd be on your way to the Bahamas by now, Malc."

"Tomorrow," he said. He didn't like the sound of this.

Bazza laughed.

"I assume you got that plank Woolley to sack most of the staff."

"Yes."

"Well he's next for the high jump. Tell him yourself since you're there. We don't want any of your staff on the premises when we take over. Break the sad news that the company has no assets so there will be no redunancy pay."

"Yes," he managed to say through the shock that was strangling him.

"Cheerio then."

He sat and stared at the telephone as if it were to blame for his misfortune. He'd heard about these asset-strippers but thought it was all exaggerated propaganda from a bunch of lefties.

Apparently not.

He was in the middle of an expensive divorce. His dear wife's solicitors had advised her to "take him to the cleaners" and he felt as if he'd been through a hot wash and spin dry.

He couldn't afford the mortgage and he had received a letter saying that if he missed another payment he would be out of house and home. Then there were the solicitors' fees to consider.

Things couldn't get this bad, not for people like him, surely?

...

"Well I can do yer 'ouse contents for yer but I can't sell a lot of this," the man looked round the room.

"I tell you what, since it's you, I think I can stretch to an 'undred smackers, waddaya say, mate?"

Councillor Woolley had spent a small fortune on the house contents but lacked haggling skills. The look of amazement on the face of the house clearance 'geezer' when he accepted the derisory offer told him that.

He had never heard of "sofa surfing" but staying with different friends for short periods was preferable to living on the streets.

He managed to get £3000 for the car. This was a seventh of the original price but it would keep him going for eight weeks.

The job hunt was not going well. The electronics industry was contracting and he was older than most other applicants. The firms wanted people who were "dynamic go-getters" and not "set in their ways." The other applicants were all cocky, self-confident and had a sense of entitlement.

"They are just like I was at twenty!" That realisation didn't cheer him up.

That evening while wearing out his welcome with a Councillor, he had this conversation;

"Tony, I am only too pleased to have you staying with us of course. How long do you think...?"

"I shall be moving on this weekend." As he said this a vision of the cold shelters on the windy sea front came to mind and he shivered.

"Well, you see, old man, there is just one thing. I know it's none of your fault of course but we have discussed it and...well to cut a long story short, we are not too happy about someone with such debts remaining on the council. It is rather letting the side down, you know."

"Yes."

"So you will be resigning by the end of the week."

It wasn't a question.

"We'll get someone else to keep an eye on that 'Project' palaver of course."

This blow led him to take a renewed interest in The Project. He got talking with one young man, let's call him Terry.

Terry was worried about a criminal charge of stealing mobile phones which would mean going back to prison.

"You see, last time it was my first stretch in Lewes Prison so I had a cell to myself. Now I won't and there are some pretty hair-raising characters in that place. I don't know what to do about it."

"Have you considered **not** stealing mobile phones?" Tony couldn't help asking.

He got a punch on the nose for his trouble.

Tony's old sleeping bag wasn't much use. The stuffing had gone out of it. He had no choice. He needed something to keep out the cold in one of the draughty "tramps' hotels" on the sea front. He didn't want to bump into Terry or his mates in the ghastly car park.

Then the money ran out completely. There was always universal credit. Although he knew it was a world-beating system, it did take a long time to get any money and meanwhile he needed food.

It was a very different Tony Woolley who turned up at The Project. The free meal was excellent, all things considered. He ate alone. It became a regular thing for him to turn up for a free meal once a day and to take his usual corner table.

He also started to be glad the council had failed to close the library. He could get a free look at the newspapers and it was warm. Without a mailing address he couldn't get a library card and that seemed unfair.

Then one day in The Project old Ron spotted him and brought his meal over to his table.

"Is it OK to sit here?"

"Well I am here for a handout, so yes."

"They have replaced you on the committee with a right plank, can't you..."

"I'm not a councillor any more."

"That's easy then, we'll co-opt you. However, before we do that there is something I want to ask you."

"Ask away."

"Are you between jobs at the moment?"

Tony actually laughed.

"You could put it like that."

"So could you find time to pop in and visit Terry in Lewes prison and take him a few things. The poor lad hasn't spoken to his family in years and he gets no visitors."

Tony hesitated, so old Ron added, "He can't punch you on the nose in prison, there's a big perspex screen."

"You persuaded me."

"And there is a job but I think you're both over qualified and under qualified. You don't need a degree but you do need to cook, we can give you training. Also you need to learn to live on minimum wage. The meals will be free of course."

"Now take your time..."

"Yes."

"Yes, you'll take your time?"

"I mean yes I'll take the job."

"The committee will decide so we won't co-opt you until after but the training can start today."

"Yes."

"And no more jokes about people getting handouts."

They shook hands.

The End

A Likely Story

"i spoke with my father last night, er and my mother," I said.

"'Er' indeed," said Martin, "you realise they are both dead?"

"Yes and no."

"What do you mean, 'yes and no'. You don't believe in ghosts do you... and if you say 'yes and no' again, this conversation is at an end."

"My father explained to me about ghosts sixty five years ago so I may not be word perfect. Ghosts, he said, are ideas in your head. When people die their souls either cease to exist or they go to heaven. In dreams and reveries, nobody really dies. I revisited my childhood home,"

"In a dream?"

"Mm Hm."

"For the tape, Derek nodded," I think my old friend Martin watches way too much detective fiction.

"My father,"

"Who died when you were seven?"

"Yes, that father. I only had the one."

"He was there, my mother was in the scullery. My wife was there too so I had to introduce her."

"Mum offered her tea and had two stabs at her name but got there in the end with some prompting."

"So what did he say?"

"That was the funny thing. He died in 1959 but he seemed to know everything which had happened after that event. We talked about LGBTQ+ equality and I expected to have to argue down his 1950s attitudes but not a bit of it. 'Homophobia is fascist,' he said. 'Full stop.'"

"He wasn't happy with the Labour Party he had supported all his life but he wasn't particularly surprised either. 'Betrayal is implicit in reformism,' he said adding, "If things don't alter they'll stop as they are.' The last bit was just an old family joke."

"Hilarious," said Martin, "Did he say anything else."

"He told me how to find you."

Martin was unusually silent at this point.

Martin went to the window and looked out at the rain.

"He told you how to find me?"

"Hm mm,"

"Well I'm damned."

"Probably," I said. That would have amused the old Martin. He essayed a smile as watery as the weather.

We chatted for a while, mainly about the past. We had been to the same school. It no longer existed but that didn't stop us talking as though old Badger was still alive and still had the school bully waiting outside his office for the cane.

"Of course, he never stopped being a bully, just a bully with a sore backside," said Martin. I agreed.

We shared a bottle of claret and in due course it was time for me to take my leave.

The next day I had a journey to Pawsons' Road, the old cemetery where we used to go to smoke during the lunch break.

I found my way to Martin's grave by trial and error, mainly error.

I lay the flowers down and said my goodbyes.

I knew it was only "au revoir," of course.

The end

Extracting Moonbeams from Cucumbers

Doctor Ambrose lived in an unremarkable house in a pretty nondescript street in an unfashionable part of town. He was anything but ordinary however.

Nobody knew where his money came from, what he was up to at any particular time and exactly what he was a doctor of.

At first we, his next-door neighbours, were mildly interested. Then we wondered. By the end we were downright nosy.

While we were sitting down to tea, there was a noise and it was definitely coming from Dr Ambrose's house. Through the party wall I could hear that it was a voice and it was a good octave higher than the doctor's. We couldn't hear any words.

The next day I loitered in the garden and casually asked,

"By the way, what are you a doctor of?"

"Philosophy," said Dr Ambrose and walked smartly away.

This is a useless answer. PhDs are awarded for many things like Physics, Chemistry or extracting moonbeams from cucumbers.

The doctor turned at the corner and raised his voice slightly, "My thesis was on extracting moonbeams from cucumbers," he said.

Mind-reading is a myth or a trick but what dastardly trick the doctor had performed I did not know.

"So what have we got so far?" I asked

"Nothing?" Sara answered unhelpfully.

"1) He calls himself doctor but what kind of doctor?, 2) What is the the source of his income and 3) He was able to say exactly what I was thinking."

"1) So what? 2) None of our business and 3) Ah," she said.

"Ah indeed."

And there we left it until a month later when I saw my old friend Declan.

"I saw an advert in the paper for a woman called Clair Voyant. That's quite a pseudonym eh. She claimed to know things about me I didn't know myself and she offered online consultations. Her rates were very reasonable."

Declan is as gullible as a herring but on with the story.

"I went online and I couldn't see her. There was just a crystal ball with a heart of fire which held my attention. Then I asked questions and she answered. I spoke but her answers came up as text. She really did tell me some amazing things."

"F'rinstance, you remember my uncle Jed?"

"Yes,"

"She asked 'did I have a relative with a name beginning with J' how amazing is that? Then she said that all his money had disappeared when he died. How could she possibly know all that? What do you think, old man?"

I kept silent and encouraged him to continue.

"You see I heard from my cousin, Jed's erm.."

"Daughter," I prompted.

"Yes, how did you know that?"

"Lucky guess, do go on."

"Anyway Selina told me that when Jed died all his money had vanished. How about that?"

I knew for a fact that most of Jed's money had vanished behind the bar of the Duck and Shovel but I kept that to myself.

I then asked one question and the answer to it got me thinking. Apparently Selina contacted Declan by email.

First I did an extensive search of my email account. Sure enough, ten years ago I had an email with the phrase "extracting moonbeams from cucumbers" as a classic example of proverbial nonsense.

I did a little discreet research into the world of cyber-security

Sara and I arranged to question "Clair Voyant" the next day.

The crystal ball was impressive and Clair answered every question about myself that I asked. When I thought I had enough written down I ended with,

"I expect this beats extracting moonbeams from cucumbers."

Silence reigned.

Now I had chapter and verse that "Clair Voyant" and Doctor Ambrose were one and the same. They had been hacking into email accounts which was a criminal offence.

I presented the evidence to the local nick and then patiently explained it.

We have new neighbours now. So has the Doctor, in Lewes Prison.

The End

The Mirror of Eternity

It is not possible to travel in time in the way HG Wells envisaged. It causes too many paradoxes. However, in the mind, it is possible to go to any place and any time. This story is a revised version of "In the Mirror of Eternity". A previous version was published in "Alternative History Fiction Magazine".

Xavier, leant back in his chair and took an improbably large swig of Châteauneuf-du-Pape. He said, "In this very pub, according to legend, Disraeli and Gladstone, both of whom went on to become prime ministers in the nineteenth century, used to drink. Disraeli was very clever and witty and Gladstone was just Gladstone."

Xavier hooked a passing waitress called Tilly with his cane to order another bottle. This was obviously a two-bottle story or more.

"As young men, these famous individuals fought a duel over a young lady called Eliza Trollope. And it is recorded that Eliza's response to their derring-do was to say, 'These fine gentlemen haven't got a clue how to behave, I won't have neither of 'em.' And she didn't."

"If only" and here Xavier had a look in his eye which suggested a story to come if I could wheedle it out of him, "if only there were some way to verify history."

At this point, he got a phone call from his father so I will take advantage of this hiatus to say that while Xavier is a technologist his father is a physicist. Once in a while, he tries to find a practical application for his father's theoretical work. I caught the phrase "sub specie aeternitatis" in the conversation. "In the mirror of eternity."

A bottle and a half later, Xavier was explaining to me as best he could the project he was working on. It was simply (or very complexly perhaps) a device for looking back into the past to ascertain whether our view of history is accurate.

He even invited me to a private viewing of this device the following week before its public unveiling to the Royal Society in October.

I was excited at the prospect despite my misgivings. I have always taken Xavier's technological expertise with a pinch of salt. He is an amusing companion and has an apparently infinite capacity for fine wine but I was a little sceptical about whether this "Mirror of Eternity" would actually work.

The procedure was that I had to take a pill beforehand and wait for thirty minutes. The time didn't drag as Xavier talked charmingly and engagingly about the book he was reading, a show he had seen and a new pub he thought we could visit later that evening.

Then I was ushered into the presence of the Mirror itself. In a plain white room with just one chair stood what looked like a plain flat-screen television.

The controls were complex but Xavier talked me through them before leaving me alone in the room.

Using the time controls I chose a point in time and using the geo setting I chose a location.

I took a leap back seventy years. In an underground bunker, two individuals were playing cards. It was difficult to see through the clouds of cigar smoke. However, I immediately recognised the faces of Winston Churchill and Adolf Hitler.

Hitler was offended by the smoke and he was continually giving a fake little cough and waving the smoke away. Churchill seemed impervious to this and carried on smoking enthusiastically.

By a slight adjustment, I was able to see their hands. Hitler was bluffing with a pair of nines while Churchill had three tens. In the middle of the table were cards with the names of countries on them. Churchill had just gambled France and Hitler threw in Poland and Austria. Churchill considered seriously and toyed briefly with cards labelled India and Burma. In the end he obviously felt that gambling the colonies would be a step too far so he threw his hand in. I tried to yell at him. In fact I did yell at him but of course he couldn't hear.

"OK you win this time. We will be out of Dunkirk by Tuesday."

-x-x-x-x-x-

I googled Disraeli and Gladstone and lurked for a while in Ye Old Boar pub in the early nineteenth century but to no avail. The only duels between those two seem to have been battles of wits in which the worthy and wordy Gladstone went down in the first round.

I went further back and further afield too. In a magnificent villa in Tuscany I saw Julius Caesar reclining on a magnificent bed. He was very old and it seemed that he was dying of old age. His lifelong friend Brutus was crying helplessly and inconsolably at his bedside. Some words were exchanged but their Latin was so dreadful I found it impossible to understand.

-x-x-x-x-x-

I went back (or forward in this case) to a time and place where English was spoken. It was a desperate situation. Bloody Hell it was desperate. I was in despair for a start. Everyone I could see was in despair or blissfully unaware of what was to come.

Perhaps the old saw is true: "If you can keep your head when all about you are losing theirs, you really haven't understood the situation."

And for all my awareness of the desperate situation, I was perfectly safe in the twenty-first century. Everyone I could see in London in 1945 was as far from safe as it is possible to be.

Hitler's atom bomb was going to be delivered to a London address via V2 in the next week. And after that, the world was going to be his radioactive oyster. Everyone I could see walking around the streets, trying to live their lives normally under extraordinary circumstances would be dead. I could do nothing. I could only watch them through the mirror of eternity.

The crowning proof that the Nazis had the atom bomb had come via the BBC that afternoon. It was a categorical official denial. Up to then, people had only known about the bomb through rumour and the broadcasts of "Lord Haw Haw". It was illegal to listen to Nazi propaganda but everybody knew somebody who knew somebody who did.

Now the idea was in the public domain and everyone in the pub was talking about the bomb as an imminent threat or were dismissing it as 'just another big bomb'. They had seen bombs which could bring the house down in one go and with any luck, it wouldn't be their house or they would be in the shelter when it fell.

According to the German broadcasts, the Third Reich had given proof they had the bomb to the governments of the UK, USA and USSR and they had said they would demonstrate its power on London unless Britain unconditionally surrendered. The deadline had come and gone.

Of course, I was safe, but I was also in no position to alter events. I went back to the present.

...

In Ye Old Boar, Xavier was making a deep impression on the Pinotage Special Reserve.

"You see 'the mirror of eternity' was just an expression, "sub specie aeternitatis" is what many people, not you obviously, but many people, use to sum up how insignificant phenomena in this world are. ""sub specie aeternitatis" your life or mine or even the fate of Bristol Rovers is not as important as we might think.

"Then it got me thinking. I actually tried to construct a mirror of eternity which would enable me to look into the past and verify history. Time travel itself of course is impossible due to Gibson's Paradox."

"Gibson's?"

"Well it was certainly somebody's, excuse me wench."

While Xavier taps a barmaid with his cane I will mention that I have often wondered why Xavier doesn't get thrown out of pubs more often.

"Is it Gibson who postulated that if you send a signal back in time from a machine in order to switch the machine off it would therefore not send the signal and therefore not be switched off?"

"Well, Xavier," she gave a weary smile, "that sounds like Xavier's paradox to me. Another bottle?"

After pouring out two generous glasses of wine, Xavier continued, "However, the breakthrough came when I happened to take some LSD. I say LSD, it was actually a concoction of my own devising."

"Xavier you are not a chemist. Was it just LSD?"

"No, you're right, I'm no chemist. It was LSD, I bought it from a little man in Clapham. He's very good. Of course I was taking a few other things at the time and I added them to what we chemists call 'the mixture'. And then I found that the mirror of eternity worked until the stuff wore off of course.

"I know you are unhappy about the victims of the nuclear attack on London in 1945 because you cannot do anything for them."

"What can I do about this unhappiness then, Xavier?"

"I am doing it," he raised his glass and indicated that I should do likewise. "This particular grape has the power to give you perspective."

"Just this one?"

"Well it is a lifetime's study, we can't expect to get through every grape in one night. And one other thing, next time go to Addington. Go to Addington a month after the atomic bomb."

-x-x-x-x-x-

The controls of the Mirror of Eternity had a "points of interest" setting So I went to the Dunscratchin Pet Cemetery in Addington.

This was as close to London as anyone was likely to go, I thought, but I had reckoned without Ernst Rohm.

I immediately recognised Hitler and Churchill. The British leader had been forced to eschew his cigars but probably thought this a small price to pay for the unlimited power his Führer was offering him over the British Empire.

A group of Storm Troopers were dressed in anti-radiation suits. It made them look more like Darth Vader's storm troopers than Rohm's to be honest. They entrained and I followed them. I reflected that the radiation wasn't going to affect me after all.

I identified Hitler's faithful right-hand man immediately because his anti-radiation suit was at least twice as big as any of his hunky followers. He had almost unlimited power to match his girth after that unfortunate altercation with the SS in 1934. It was rumoured that he kept Heinrich Himmler on as an office boy and occasional (allegedly unwilling) sexual partner.

Although Hitler had sufficient regard to his safety to keep well away from the smoking ruins of London, Rohm said that he felt the hand of history on his shoulder and was prepared to deputise for his Führer on this occasion, taking the salute outside the remains of the Houses of Parliament – or "relic of decadent democracy" as he preferred to call it.

Rohm's speech was incomprehensible (with apologies to any German speakers among my readers).

The view was eloquent enough. In every direction, the city had been levelled. Overhead there was a squadron of Spitfires with new German markings. They were braving the radiation to make a point.

As I used the altitude setting to join the lead plane I expected to see fat Herman in the cockpit. What I saw was a sleek fit Herman Goering reliving his glory days as a fighter pilot. The flight started doing manoeuvres that the Spitfire is definitely not designed to do and getting away with it too.

The last thing I saw was a big smile on Goering's lips as he said – apparently to me but that was impossible - "next time New York"

My ears were ringing with him singing "We'll take Manhattan, the Bronx and Staten Island too."

-x-x-x-x-x-

There followed a pause as Xavier was arrested for possession of banned substances. He tried in vain to convince the court that he was conducting scientific research and received a massive fine and a suspended sentence.

I met him in the antechamber to the courtroom among various drunks, child molesters and licence fee dodgers. He wasn't going to discuss the case. He was going to discuss the cat.

He was under the impression that Gibson had tortured cats until they confessed that they felt very uncertain about everything. It was a toss-up whether to tell him that it was Schrödinger and the exact nature of the experiment or to let it go.

"In any case," he said, taking a large swig from a hip flask, "he was entirely wrong. You don't alter the nature of phenomena by observing them. It's a solipsism.

He gave me a very broad hint as to where I should go next when he was back in funds.

-x-x-x-x-x-

It was a cold day in Moscow in March 1933 although I couldn't feel it. The room in the Kremlin was furnished in an austere style.

The walls were virtually undecorated apart from a portrait of a young Joseph Stalin bordered with a black ribbon. This commemorated his untimely death in 1918 when he bravely or accidentally took a bullet from Fanya Kaplan which was intended for Lenin.

The other wall decoration was a map which showed the USSR had incorporated most of Asia with the exception of Ceylon. This was drawn to my attention by one of the three men in the room.

This was Victor Serge. Fortunately for me (my Russian is on a par with my German) his presence meant the discussion was mainly conducted in French.

"So in conclusion, the government has asked for admission to the USSR and outlined this program of economic assistance."

The other two men looked cursorily at the paperwork, turned to the bottom line, frowned and then shrugged.

"Well it will have to go to the Central Committee but realistically this is a small price to pay for terminating the British Empire." Lenin seemed grimly satisfied with the outcome but there was another problem occupying his mind.

He turned to the other man in the room, "OK Leon, Germany."

The People's Commissar for War, Lev Davidovich Trotsky, couldn't resist standing up. A look from Lenin said loud and clear- "Just the facts, we don't need a speech."

"The problem we all know. Together the Social Democrats and the Communist Party outnumber the Nazis. Hitler can never come to power."

"However, the Social Democrats have been selling their principles wholesale. They betrayed the revolution of 1919 and they have sought to have Rosa Luxemburg assassinated on five separate occasions before she sought asylum here.

"So how are we to unite against the Nazis and can we trust the SDP to fight them anyway?"

He waited for an answer but the others knew him too well so he continued.

"Over the last six months a steady stream of members have been leaving the CP to join the Social Democrats. In all about ten thousand. Need I tell you that they were doing this under our instructions?

"On Tuesday Ernst Thälmann will propose to the German CP conference that the organisation be dissolved and members should aid the Social Democrats to resist the Nazis.

We calculate the Social Democrats – who have been calling for this measure – will find it hard to oppose it. Within a month we should be able to present the German people with something they have never seen before,. Social Democrats with backbone."

There was a lot of discussion about how this could be achieved but I didn't need to listen to it.

-x-x-x-x-

Forward to Tuesday. A packed hall in Berlin. Armed guards from the Red Front patrolled outside and kept the stormtroopers at bay. Few people could resist the rhetoric of Thälmann when he was in full flow but in the event he didn't need to persuade the conference.

The guest speaker, who had been sent on a sealed train from exile in Russia, was Rosa Luxemburg. Trotsky had persuaded her, God alone knew how, to support the liquidation of the German Communist Party for the greater good.

The subsequent election was a foregone conclusion. In panic, Britain and America had poured millions into the Nazi Party funds but it was no use.

President Thälmann applied to join the USSR by the end of the year. And the economic package he suggested was one nobody needed to frown over.

Hitler went back to house painting.

"You see," said Xavier waving a wine bottle as if he were conducting an orchestra. "Britain has always been part of the USSR. You can't change history just by going back and looking at it."

He held up the bottle in a signal to the barmaid that it was time for another.

The End

This is the second story in the Twitten series.

Ragamuffin's Boot

Eric Twitten was enjoying a drink at The Lamb in Durrington. He was in the habit of taking his cross-breed dog, Ragamuffin, with him. Ragamuffin usually occupied the space in front of the fire and the landlord was minded to ban him from the pub.

"Now look here," he said to Eric.

Then he noticed Ragamuffin looking at him as if he were a tasty morsel he might have for his tea.

He changed the subject.

"Hey, what has your dog got there?"

Eric looked. Ragamuffin had picked up a boot from somewhere and was guarding it with two paws while taking the occasional nibble.

"Anybody missing a boot?" Eric asked.

None of the regulars was missing a boot.

"He must have picked it up on the way here," Eric concluded.

Ragamuffin took the boot back home in his mouth as if it were a new-born puppy.

"You are not bringing that filthy old boot in my clean kitchen," was Peggy's verdict. The boot had to remain outside until Eric had washed and dried it.

Ragamuffin greeted it like a long-lost friend. He walked around the house with it, much to Peggy's impotent disgust.

From then on, whenever Eric and Ragamuffin went for a walk, which was every day, old boot had to come too, firmly held in Ragamuffin's somewhat slobbery jaws.

Peggy made it clear that it was not coming on her weekly shopping expeditions.

Ragamuffin protested.

Peggy made as though to leave him behind.

He dropped the old boot.

The co-op was right next door to the Lamb so Ragamuffin could have made his way there with his eyes closed.

Peggy had to leave him tied up outside and (don't tell Eric) she always left him with something to chew, a bone or a pig's ear, while she did the weekly shop.

"What have you got there, Ragamuffin?" she asked when she had finished the shopping and caught up on the Durrington gossip.

Ragamuffin tried to conceal his find.

"It's another boot!" Peggy concluded. "There's something odd about this. It looks just the same as t'other which means they are both right boots and not a pair."

When she got home and washed and dried the boot, only to have Ragamuffin slobber all over it when he got it back, her suspicion was confirmed.

Eric and Peggy both had a go at guessing the story behind Ragamuffin's boots but the truth was rather strange.

The public bar of the Lamb was an all-male affair in those days. Once a man had tried to bring his girl friend in but he had been diverted to the saloon bar with a flea in his ear.

They all knew each other. Although Eric was an incomer, he was more-or-less accepted because he didn't mind standing a round of drinks once in a while. They accepted him. They also accepted the drinks.

So the arrival of a stranger was something of an event.

The man slouched awkwardly up to the bar, aware that everybody was watching him. He leant heavily on a crutch. He counted his money and had just enough for a half pint of bitter.

With a glass in his hand, he had the confidence to look around the bar and acknowledge the hard stares of the locals with an easy grin.

When he got to Ragamuffin, he stopped. He walked over to the dog, who didn't seem to mind. He patted his head and turned to the company with the air of a man with a story to tell. If you can't buy a round of drinks, tell a good yarn.

"A fine dog, What's his name, may I ask?"

"Ragamuffin."

"A good tough name for a good tough dog, I'll warrant."

Eric smiled at this. Peggy had chosen the name but it was a very suitable one.

"Well your Ragamuffin has got something of mine. Mind you I don't begrudge it."

Now he had everyone's attention.

"That's my old right boot, you see."

Nobody asked how he had come to lose it so he stamped on the floor with his wooden leg to make the point.

"Yes, I lost my leg to a blasted French cannon ball so I don't begrudge Ragamuffin here of any of my shoes he might take a fancy to."

The company bought him all the drinks he could possibly want while he told his war stories and they talked about the bloody French, the blasted French and the bastard French in the somewhat repetitive manner of a bar crowd.

Eric chanced upon the stranger later that evening as they wandered unsteadily from the Lamb. The stranger approached him confidentially.

"Eric, Eric, Eric, you're my bes' friend in the whole wassname. I tell you what, I tell you what, I tell you what,"

Eric was beginning to wonder what was "what", then the stranger continued.

"You don't need to mind my stories, Eric. I'm away to Goring in the morning so I may as well tell you the truth. You see I lost my leg in a common or garden wassname, you know 'dustrial accident. Nobody'll buy you a drink and think you an excelent fellow if you tell them about that."

"If you liked my war stories, mind, I'll be telling the good folk at the Mulberry all about them tomorrow night."

Eric wished him goodnight.

From then on, Ragamuffin had to decide which boot he was taking with him when they went for a walk. He tried to hold on to both of them but even his mouth wasn't quite up to the task.

The end

The best of pies

Kaspar, a newcomer, was holding forth at Xavier's table in Ye Olde Boar. "It was the best of pies. It was the worst of pies. I have to admit the pastry could not be faulted. I actually enjoyed it. Then as soon as I bit into the pie I found that it was all gristle and bits of animal I prefer not to speculate about."

There were several sympathetic noises around the table as Kaspar continued, "The Commanding Officer stood over me and made sure I ate every scrap of it too. I noticed that all of the troops who were going out to the forward base ate these pies. It was as if it were some kind of toughening-up exercise.

"I was there," (*I should mention that Kaspar was a journalist formerly employed by The Dictator*) "to report on the victory over the hill tribes who had been revolting.

The Dictator was going to defeat them in the next four days. If there were no victory there would be no report. The CO cheerily told me not to worry about it because in that case I would probably be dead anyway. He actually slapped me on the back quite hard and the officers who were sitting at the table with me found it quite amusing.

"Orders were shouted and echoed around this dreadful underground bunker where we had been eating. As we were leaving a subaltern pointed out the steel doors to me.

"'They will hold out for a good four days.' was his confident prediction. If I had any trepidation about the food at the forward base, i

t was immediately dispelled at my next meal. The food was plentiful and better than I have ever tasted at any army base. The men visibly perked up. Life at the forward base might be a little fraught. Correction, it **was** fraught, what with snipers and improvised explosive devices going off every five minutes. However the food and the conditions were excellent. Nothing like the horror pie of my first night came my way again.

"It was on the second day that the hill tribesmen launched an assault on the camp. I have seen better attacks mounted by unarmed Boy Scouts to be honest with you but the CO gave the order "panic stations" and the men retreated in disorder.

"The soldiers held on to their guns for the most part but I noticed that they dropped their packs in order to move the faster. The disciplined troops looked like a complete and utter rabble. I expected the CO to be incandescent with rage. On the contrary I caught sight of him smiling at the panic. The hill tribesmen were so busy looting the abundant supplies in the camp they were slow to give chase and the steel doors of the underground redoubt clanged behind us.

"The CO did a piece to camera for me. 'We have just fought a decisive engagement with the rebels and they will give us no trouble for many years to come. The casualties among the hill tribesmen have been catastrophic while as you can see,' (a quick pan around the room) 'all of my men are unharmed.'

"I was baffled. The CO went back to his office with senior officers and a bottle of Scotch. For the rest of us it was the ghastly pies again. To my surprise I saw a number of pies being taken into the CO's office as well.

"Four days later when the steel doors opened again, the hills were eerily silent except for the sound of carrion crows. The forward base and two villages I visited were littered with remains. None of the rebels or their wives and children had a mark on them but it was clear that they had died in agony.

"'Poison?' I asked somewhat incredulously, 'our supplies were all poisoned? So we were eating poison the whole time?'

The CO just nodded.

"'And the pies?' I asked.

The CO told me that I needed to eat one every four days or so. They were vile so that any which fell into the wrong hands were unlikely to be eaten but they did contain the antidote.

The poison takes roughly four days to work as I could see. I was allowed to report the victory but there were to be no details of how it was achieved, just in case we decided to use this method again. It is the Dictator's own idea of course. He is a strong man."

There was a silence around the table after that. We were used to Xavier's tall tales but Kaspar's story had the ring of truth about it.

The end

What to do next

If you have enjoyed this book, please feel free to write a glowing review on Amazon.

Then you should try your hand at writing flash fiction. You might like to start with a story of 100 words.

There is an annual 100-word challenge on #worthingflash and the rules are very simple. The story should be 100 words or fewer.

We are surrounded by stories, everything from the parables in the Bible to those jokes which begin "a man walked into a pub." Your story could be somewhere between the two!

https://worthingflash.blogspot.com .

Email your story to worthingflash@gmail.com .

Printed in Great Britain
by Amazon

84255163R00047